STORIES
OF
THE STEPPE

STORIES OF THE STEPPE

by

MAXIM GORKI

TRANSLATED BY
HENRY T. SCHNITTKIND :: ISAAC GOLDBERG

Short Story Index Reprint Series

 BOOKS FOR LIBRARIES PRESS
FREEPORT, NEW YORK

First Published 1918
Reprinted 1970

STANDARD BOOK NUMBER:
8369-3508-X

LIBRARY OF CONGRESS CATALOG CARD NUMBER:
72-121552

PRINTED IN THE UNITED STATES OF AMERICA

Introduction

MAXIM GORKI, the Bitter Voice of Russia, can tell fairy tales whose coloring has all the richness of oriental twilights and whose cadences are garlands woven of sea-spray and wind-blossoms. His stories of the steppe are not propagandistic, and with the exception of the powerful tale *Because of Monotony*, they are not sordid pictures of realistic misery, but they are sweet fairy lullabies that the gods must sing to the baby angels when they are sad and weary with their contemplation of human sorrows. These tales are filled with longing, and throughout that longing there is a thread of red fire that at times bursts forth into a flaming prophecy of hope. Perhaps Gorki, in writing those strange, wonderfully magical fairy tales, was unconsciously rehearsing that strangest and most wonderful fairy tale of them all,— the great Russian Revolution.

He who has no love for music had better leave these stories alone, as they will have no charm for him. He who prefers society to sunsets will find these stories dull and colorless,— as colorless as the clouds at the close of the day are to a blind man. But those who have the capacity for enjoying the silent music of the night, the barely audible purling of sea-waves in the distance, the soft pit-a-pat of the wind-dance on the prairie, will be charmed by these stories as they have rarely been charmed in their waking hours. For these stories of the steppe have all the magic of dreams; their atmosphere envelopes you and permeates your every pore, sinking deep into your heart through every one of your five senses, and through a sixth sense, too,— a sense whose very indefinable vagueness makes it the most vivid of them all. For it is that sense,— or shall I call it religious experience,— which enables you to realize eternity in the single

INTRODUCTION

tick of a clock and infinity in a drop of water. It is that sense which sometimes catches you unawares, as you pass on your prosaic road of jagged experiences between a dream and a dream, when suddenly turning your head, you see God nodding and smiling to you as he pauses for an instant in this labor of creating new worlds.

The Russians, we are told, are dreamers. Fortunate Russians! The greatest and finest and most enduring things in the world are the handiwork of dreamers. Men of action who are unable to dream are the destroyers of the world; they are the Hindenburgs, the Hohenzollerns, those brute forces that cannot leave their imprint on the sands of time unless the sand is soaked in human blood. It is the dreamers, men like Gorki and Tolstoi, who out of the elements of sea and land can build a fairy tale and out of the chaos of tyranny and suffering can create a nation of free men and women.

Maxim Gorki is one of the supreme dreamer-revolutionists of the present day, and the stories of the steppe are among his most wonderful visions. The translators have been rather free in their rendering, for it has required the utmost care to reproduce the tang and the perfume of the Russian steppe on American soil. A dream of such fine coloring and melody can be totally shattered by the introduction of the slightest jarring note, and the translators hope that at least a fraction of the beauty of the original has been preserved in this version.

H. T. S.

CONTENTS

	PAGE
MAKAR CHUDRA	9
BECAUSE OF MONOTONY	27
THE MAN WHO COULD NOT DIE	49

Makar Chudra

A MOIST and chilly wind carried over the steppe the melancholy murmur of the waves that splashed against the shore, and of the shrubbery which covered the water's edge. Now and then the wind drove before it a multitude of withered yellow leaves, whirling them into the camp-fire and fanning its flames, whereupon a shudder crept over the darkness that enveloped us, piercing the autumn night and revealing to the left— the limitless steppe, and to the right—the infinite ocean against the background of which crouched the figure of Makar Chudra, an old gypsy who had been set to watch over the horses of the camp which was situated about fifty paces from us.

He seemed utterly unconscious of the cold blasts of the wind that whipped open his gypsy cloak, exposing and lashing unmercifully his hairy bronze-colored chest. Turning toward me his free, strong and handsome face from his recumbent posture, he thoughtfully puffed away at his big pipe, blowing thick clouds of smoke from his mouth and nostrils. His motionless eyes were fixed beyond me upon the darkness that stretched endlessly over the death-like silence of the steppe. He talked to me without interruption, making no motion whatsoever to shield himself against the pitiless buffeting of the storm.

"And so you are joining us? That's fine! You have chosen a splendid course, Falcon. We all have to meet our fate. Go about and see the world, and when you have seen enough, lie down and die— and that's all!

"Life? Other people?" he continued — "H'm! What business is it of yours? Are you not yourself a slice of life? And as for other people, they have been living without you and they will continue to live without you. Do you think anybody needs you? You're neither bread nor a staff; why then should people have need of you?

"To learn and to teach, you say? Can you ever learn how to make people happy? No, you can't. You will only become gray and then you will say that you must teach others. But what are you going to teach them? Everybody knows what he needs. The wise take everything, the fools get nothing, and everybody learns for himself...

"Human beings are ridiculous, crowding themselves together into a single heap and stifling the life out of one another, when there is so much room in the world," — he extended his hand toward the wide steppe. — "And they are forevermore working. For what? For whom? Nobody knows. You behold a man at the plough, and you think: First he wastes away his strength tilling the earth by the sweat of his brow, and then he stretches his own corpse in it and rots away. Nothing remains of him, he does not even reap his own sowing, but dies just as he was born, a blockhead.

"Can it be that he is born for this,—to dig about in the earth and then to die even before he has succeeded in preparing his own grave? Has he known freedom? Does he understand the wide expanse of the steppe? The multitudinous murmur of the sea, is his heart ever gladdened by that sound? H'm! From the moment of his birth he is a slave, and throughout all his life he remains a slave, that's all! He can do nothing to help himself, except to put a noose around his head if ever he becomes a little wiser.

"But as for me — just look at me, will you — I have seen so much in my fifty odd years that if I were to write it all down on paper, it would fill more than a thousand sacks like the one you've got there. Yes, and then there would be some left over. I'd like you to show me the country I haven't been to. Why, you haven't even *heard* of all the countries I have visited. That's the way to live — wandering, wandering, — staying only for a little while in each place. — Why not? Just as the day and the night are forever on the go, chasing each other around the earth, I would advise you to be on the move, away from your thoughts about life, if you don't want to get sick of them. For the more you think of life the less you like it, that's how it always happens. I, too, have had the same experience. Yes, Falcon, I've lived through it all myself.

"I have been in jail; it was in Galicia, and I had plenty of time to philosophize there. What am I in this world for? I used to ask myself. I would get these thoughts into my head just to break the monotony,—for it certainly was monotonous there! At such moments my heart was oppressed with longing whenever I looked at the fields through the prison bars. My heart was pressed as in a vise!... Yes, Falcon, we live in this world and that is all. Who knows why? Nobody. And it's useless to ask. Live and live fully; keep wandering and look about you, and you will never long for that which you haven't got, never! At that time I could have strangled myself with my girdle. Yes, Falcon, I've been through it all!

"H'm! Once I spoke to a man... He was a stern fellow, — one of you, a Russian. He said: 'You ought to live not as you like, but as God has ordained. Only throw yourself at God's feet and He will give you everything that you pray for.' And yet this chap himself wore a ragged suit full of holes. I told him to get a new suit of clothes with his prayers, whereupon he became angry, cursed and drove me away from him. Up to that time he had been preaching forgiveness and love. He should therefore have forgiven me when I offended his pride with my words. There's a teacher for you! They teach you to eat less, and they themselves eat ten times a day..."

He spat into the fire and became silent, filling his pipe once more. The wind had died down to a soft, melancholy wail, the horses neighed in the darkness, and from the camp floated the tender, yet sorrowful tones of a dirge. The singer was the beautiful Nonka, the daughter of Makar. I recognized the rich and round quality of her voice which always sounded so pathetic, so full of longing and discontent — whether she were singing a song or merely saying "good morning." In her brown lustreless features you could see the smoldering hauteur of a queen and in her dark-brown eyes that were always veiled with a shadow of sadness flashed the conscious power of her charm and the irresistible attractiveness of her beauty, as well as her contempt for everything that was unlike herself.

Makar handed the pipe to me.

"Have a smoke! Doesn't the girl sing well? Don't you think so, hey? How would you like to be loved by a girl like her? You wouldn't? That's fine! You are quite right. Put no trust in women, and keep away from them. To kiss a girl is better and pleasanter than to smoke my pipe... But once you have kissed a woman the freedom of your heart is dead. A woman binds you to her with bonds that can neither be seen nor torn asunder. You give your whole soul away and you get nothing in return. Take my advice; beware of women. They are always lying, the snakes... 'I love you more than anything else in the world,' she says. And yet, if you but prick her accidentally with a pin, she will tear your heart out. I know! Ye gods, how well I know! If you will listen to me, Falcon, I'll tell you a story. But above all, be on your guard, and you will remain a free bird all your life.

"There was one upon a time a young gypsy, and his name was Zobar, Loyko Zobar. All Hungary and Bohemia and Slavonia and all the country that borders on the sea knew him, for he was a brave lad. There was not a village in the entire land in which there were not at least a dozen people who had sworn an oath to Heaven that they would kill Loyko. And yet he lived. If he ever took a fancy to a horse, he would gallop away with it even if an entire regiment had been set to watch over the beast. H'm! He feared neither God nor man. And even if Satan himself were to array his whole hellish army against him, he would oppose them single-handed, and I haven't the slightest doubt in the world that Satan's jaw would feel the taste of Zobar's mighty fist.

"And every gypsy camp knew him either by sight or by hearsay. He loved only horses, nothing else, and even these he loved only for a while. One gallop and he was done with them. And the money that he got for selling them anybody could have for the asking. He had nothing that he was unwilling to share with others. If you were to ask for his very heart, he would tear it out of his breast and give it to you for the mere pleasure of doing you a favor. That's the kind of a man he was, Falcon!

"Our band was at that time wandering through Bukowina— it was about ten years ago—. Once, in the springtime—I remember it as though it happened yesterday— we were resting; myself, Danila, the soldier who had fought with Kossuth, old Nur and all the others. Radda, Danila's daughter, was with us, too.

"You know my Nonka, don't you? Isn't she a queen of a girl! But Radda must not be compared with her, for that would be too much honor for Nonka! Words cannot describe this Radda. One might, perhaps, express her loveliness by means of the violin, but he alone could do it who knows the violin as he knows his own soul.

"Many a brave young heart did she ruin, ye gods, how many! Once a rich old man beheld her. When his glance fell upon her, he stopped as if paralyzed. He sat upon his mount and gazed at her, trembling as in a fever. He was as handsome as the devil on a holiday, his mantle was embroidered with gold, and whenever the horse stamped with his hoofs, the sabre flashed like lightning at his side... The entire sabre was inlaid with precious stones, and the bright blue velvet on his cap was like a piece of sky... A mighty nobleman was he! He gazed and gazed upon Radda, and then he said to her: 'Give me a kiss and I will give you a purse full of money in return!' She merely turned away, and that was all. 'Pardon me! Even if I have offended you, you will at least favor me with your smile, won't you?' Thus did he humble his pride, throwing a purse of money at her feet — a great, big purse, brother! But Radda merely kicked it with her foot into the dusty road, and that was all.

"'Aha! Is that the kind of a girl you are?' muttered the rich man, whipping his horse. Only a cloud of dust remained behind.

"And the next day he came again.— 'Who is her father?' he cried in a loud voice that resounded throughout the camp. Danila came. 'Sell me your daughter, and set your own price!' But Danila replied: 'This is the custom only among gentlemen; they sell everything, from their pigs to their conscience. But I have fought under Kossuth, and I will not sell anything!' The nobleman flew into a rage and grasped the hilt of his sabre, but just at that moment one of us stuck a burning match into the ear of his horse and drove him away together with the rider... We broke up our camp and wandered on. We wandered for two days, and yet he overtook us! 'Hey, you folks,' he said, 'before you and before God my conscience is clear. Give me this girl for my wife, and I will share everything with you. I am very rich!' — He was burning with excitement and just as a blade of grass quivers in the tempest, just so did he sway in the saddle.

"'Well, my daughter, speak!' grumbled Danila into his beard.

"'If the daughter of an eagle were to go of her own free will into the nest of a raven, what would she become then?' asked Radda.

"Danila laughed and we laughed with him.

" 'Well spoken, little daughter! Have you heard, your Honor? It can't be done! You had better look for a little dove —they are more submissive.'

"And we went on. The nobleman took his cap, threw it upon the ground and galloped away,—he galloped so fast that the earth quaked. That's the kind of a girl she was, Falcon!

"Yes, and one evening we were sitting and listening. Music floated over the steppe. It was a wonderful music! It set the blood in our veins afire and seemed to call us somewhere. And we, every one of us, felt as though that music awoke in us a vague longing, either to die or else to live as the ruler of the entire world. That's the kind of music it was, Falcon!

"And it came nearer and ever nearer. And suddenly a horse steps out of the darkness, and upon this horse sits a man playing on a fiddle as he approaches us. At the campfire he halts, stops playing and greets us with a smile.

" 'Ah, Zobar, it is you!' cried Danila joyously.

"That, then, was Loyko Zobar! The ends of his mustache hung way down over his shoulders, mingling together with his steel-brown locks; his eyes glittered as the bright-stars, and the very sun was mirrored in his laughter, so help me God! He looked as though chiselled out, chiselled out of one piece together with his horse. He sat as though wholly suffused with blood in the light of the glowing logs, and his teeth flashed when he laughed. May I be cursed if I did not fall in love with him immediately, even before he spoke a single word or even noticed that I, too, lived on the face of the earth!

"Yes, Falcon, that's the kind of people we sometimes find in the world! He looks into your eyes and he captures your whole soul. And you are not even ashamed of it; on the contrary, you feel proud of it. In your dealings with such a man you become better yourself. My friend, the world has not many people like him! And it is only right that this should be so. If there were much good in the world, people would no longer consider it good. That's how it is! But hear what happened after that.

"Radda spoke up: 'You play beautifully, Loyko. Who made you this fiddle with such rich full tones?'

"Loyko laughed. 'I myself have made it! Not out of wood have I made it, but out of the breast of a young girl whom I have loved ardently, and the strings have I fashioned by intertwining her heart-strings. It is still somewhat false, this fiddle, but I know how to master it with the bow in my hand. Do you see?'

"We gypsies, as you know, try from the very outset to becloud the eyes of women in order that they may not set our hearts aflame, but that they should themselves instead be filled with longing for us. Loyko acted likewise. But he struck the wrong party. Radda turned away and said, yawning: 'H'm! And yet people have told me that Loyko is wise and clever. The people have lied to me!' Saying this, she went off.

"'Aha, my beauty! You have sharp teeth!' exclaimed Loyko with flashing eyes as he jumped off his horse. 'Hail, comrades! Here I am!'

"'Be our welcome guest, O eagle!' replied Danila. After our mutual embraces we conversed for a while and then we all went to sleep... We slept soundly... The next morning we noticed that Zobar had tied a bandage around his head. What was the matter? Why, his temple had been wounded by the horse's hoof, he said.

"H'm! We knew what sort of a horse it was and we all snickered into our beards. Danila also smiled. What? Wasn't Loyko worthy of Radda? Surely not that! A girl may be as beautiful as the day, and yet her soul remains mean and cramped, and even if you hang a sackful of gold around her neck, she can never become better than she was in the first place. Yes, siree!

"Thus we lived on and on in that place. Business was good,

and Zobar remained with us. That was a comrade for you, Falcon! Wise as an old man, and skilled in everything; he even understood how to read and write Russian and Hungarian. Whenever he began to speak, you felt as though you would like to banish sleep forever just so you might listen to him! And he could play—may a thunderbolt strike me down this very moment if this world has ever seen another man who could play like Zobar. When he first drew his bow across the strings your heart began to go pit-a-pat, at the second chord your heart stopped beating. But he would play on and smile at us. We wanted to laugh and cry at the same time when we listened to his tunes. Now you could hear a long-drawn-out prayer for help that would cut your heart like a knife, with its pathos. And now the instrument reëchoed with the melody of the steppe telling fairy tales, oh such melancholy fairy-tales, to heaven. Then resounded a maiden's tearful syllables, as she was bidding farewell to her heart's beloved. And then rippled forth the cheerful laughter of her brave lover, calling her into the steppe. And suddenly, heigho! A free and lively tune leapt from his bow like a cataract, and it seemed as if the very sun would begin to dance in the heavens to the rhythm of that tune! That's the kind of music it was, Falcon!

"Every nerve in your body tingled at the sound of that music and you became its utter slave. And if Loyko had exclaimed at such a moment, 'To arms, comrades!' we would all have plunged our knives into the heart of him who might be indicated by Loyko. He could do everything with us, and we loved him, we loved him ardently. Only Radda paid no attention to him. That wouldn't have been so bad, but she even made sport of him. As in a vise she held Zobar's heart imprisoned. Loyko gnashed his teeth and twirled his long mustache. His eyes were blacker than an abyss, and yet now and then they flashed so fiercely that our hearts were filled with trembling. At night he went far into the steppe, did this fearless Loyko, and he let his fiddle wail till the dawning of the day. The fiddle wailed because his freedom was dead. And we lay awake in our camp, thinking, 'What's to be done?' We knew very well that when two rocks roll upon each other it is death to stand between them. That's how it was, Falcon!

"One day we were all sitting together and speaking about our business. Our talk was becoming monotonous and so Danila spoke up: 'Sing us a song, Zobar! Gladden our hearts with a tune!' The latter cast a glance toward Radda, who lay upon her back not far from us, her face upturned toward the sky, and then he began to draw his bow. Hereupon the fiddle started to talk, as though it really were the heart of a young girl! And Loyko sang:

> 'Ho! My heart is aflame as I ride,
> Through the wastes of the steppe so wide.
> Like an arrow flies my steed
> Shod with the whirlwind's speed.'

"Radda turned her head, raised herself on her elbow and smiled into Loyko's eyes. His face flamed up like the sunrise.

> 'Heigho! Let us gallop away
> From the night to the gates of the day!
> Let us scatter the mantle of mist
> Where the hills by the sunrise are kissed.
>
> We will ride with the sun till the night
> And spatter the sky with her light;
> We will leap into midnight from noon
> And rest on the tip of the moon.'

"That's the way he sang! Nobody can sing like that nowadays! Radda, however, merely remarked as though she were spilling water through a sieve: 'I wouldn't fly so high if I were you, Loyko. You're liable to fall down and stick your nose into a puddle, and then your mustache will get dirty. You had better look out!' Loyko glared at her for a moment, but said nothing. Controlling his rage, he continued his song:

> 'Heigho! And to-morrow will peep
> And will find us fast asleep.
> And then we will both pass away,
> In the flaming sun's red spray.'

" 'That's what I call a song!' said Danila.— 'Never in my life have I heard such a song. May Satan make a pipe out of me this very minute if I'm not telling the truth!' Old Nur stroked his mustache and shrugged his shoulders. This song of Zobar's had touched the hearts of us all. But Radda was not pleased with it.

" 'A fly once buzzed just like this when he tried to imitate the cry of the eagle,' she said. We all felt as though she had just showered us with snow.

" 'Perhaps you would like to taste the whip, Radda,' said her father. But Zobar threw his cap on the ground and with flashing eyes exclaimed: 'Stop, Danila! A fiery horse needs a bit of steel! I want your consent to marry your daughter!'

" 'Well spoken!' smiled Danila. 'Take her, if only you are willing and able!'

" 'Very well,' replied Loyko, and turned to Radda: 'Well, my pretty lass, listen to me and don't be so haughty! I have known many of your sisters, yes, many of them. But not one of them has so fired my heart as you. Ah, Radda, you have imprisoned my soul... Well, then, what am I to do about it? Whatever must happen will happen... Yes, there isn't a horse in the world who can carry you away from yourself! I ask you to marry me before God, my honor, your father and all these people. But beware of interfering with my freedom—for I am a free man and I want to live as I choose!' Hereupon, compressing his lips, he approached her. With flashing eyes he stepped forward to take her... 'Aha,' we said to ourselves, 'at last Radda has put the bit into the mouth of the steed of the steppe. But suddenly we saw him throw his hands into the air and fall down flat on his back!...

"He fell as though struck with a bullet. How had it happened? It was Radda. She had coiled the whip around his legs drawing it sharply toward herself, whereupon Loyko fell to the ground.

"And then she lay down again and looked smilingly at the sky. We waited to see what Loyko would do. The latter, however, sat on the ground pressing his temples with his hands, as though fearful that his head would burst. Then he rose quietly and went off into the steppe without casting a single glance in our direction. Nur whispered to me, 'Watch him!' And I crept after Zobar into the steppe, into the darkness of the night. That's the way it was, Falcon!..."

Makar shook the ashes out of his pipe and filled it anew.

I cuddled up in my cloak and looked into Makar's old face that was blackened by the wind and sun. Sternly and thoughtfully he shook his head, murmuring something I could not hear; his thick gray mustache trembled in the wind which played through his dishevelled hair. He resembled an old oak which, though struck by lightning, still stands tall and mighty in its invincible pride. The sea and the shore whispered interminably together, and the wind carried their whisperings over the steppe. Nonka was no longer singing and the clouds that now covered the sky made the autumn night even more dark and terrible.

"Loyko walked slowly, step by step, with bowed head and hands hanging limp and lifeless. Coming to the ravine near the river, he sat down on a rock and moaned. So piteously did he moan that my heart bled in sympathy. And yet I did not come near him. Words cannot console a man's sufferings, can they?.. Yes, he sat thus for one hour, two hours, three hours—he sat motionless near the river.

"I lay on the ground at no great distance. The night was bright, the moon threw a silvery glitter over the whole steppe, so that it was possible to see everything.

"Suddenly I see Radda walking quickly from the gypsy camp toward Loyko. I was happy, oh, so happy! After all, Radda was a most wonderful girl! She approached him, but he did not hear her. She put her hand on his shoulder. Loyko started, took his hands away from his face and raised his head. And you should have seen how he sprang to his feet and grasped the hilt of his knife! 'He will kill the girl!' I said to myself. I was just on the point of running to the camp in order to summon help when I heard these words: 'Throw it away, or else I will blow your brains out! Do you see this?' And Radda pointed a pistol at Zobar's head. That's the devil of a girl she was, Falcon! 'Now,' thought I, 'they are equally matched. What will happen next, I wonder?'

"'Listen to me!' Radda put the pistol into her belt and continued: 'I have come not to kill you but to make peace. Throw away that knife!' He threw it away and looked at her darkly. It was wonderful, brother! Here stood two creatures looking at each other like beasts of prey, and yet they were both such brave and splendid people. Only the bright moon beheld them, and I... Nobody else.

"'Now listen to me, Loyko. I love you!' He merely shrugged his shoulders, as though he were tied hand and foot.

"'I have seen many a lad, but you are braver and handsomer than all the rest. The others would all shave off their mustache at a single glance from my eye, they would all fall at my feet, if I should only ask it. But of what use would it be? With all that they could not please me, and I would only make women out of them. There are very few brave gypsies in the world, very few, Loyko. None of them have I ever loved before, but now I love you. And yet I love my freedom, and this, Loyko, I love more than you. But without you I cannot live, even as you cannot live without me. And therefore I want you to be mine, with your whole heart and soul. Do you hear?'

"He smiled. 'I hear! My heart is glad to hear your words. Speak on!'

" 'I have this much to say yet, Loyko: Whatever you do, I will compel you to become mine. And therefore I would advise you to lose no time, for my kisses and embraces are awaiting you —and most ardent will they be, these kisses and embraces of mine, Loyko! In the warmth of my arms you will forget your courageous life, and your beautiful songs that give so much joy to the gypsy folk will no longer reëcho in the steppe... You will sing only tender love songs to me, your Radda... Lose no time, therefore, but do as I say. To-morrow you must submit to me as to a superior officer. You will bow down at my feet, in the presence of the whole camp, and you will kiss my right hand— and then I will become your wife!'

"So that's what the devilish girl wanted. It was amazing. Such things had happened only in olden times, among Montenegrins, but among the gypsies, never. Submission to a woman! Tell me, Falcon, can you imagine anything more ridiculous? Why, you won't be able to do so in a hundred years. No, siree!

"Loyko sprang to his feet and uttered a cry that rang through the whole steppe, as though a bullet had just passed through his breast. Radda trembled, but did not lose her nerve.

" 'Farewell till to-morrow, and to-morrow you will do what I have commanded. Do you hear, Loyko?'

" 'I hear! I will do it!' groaned Zobar, holding his arms out to her. But she turned away from him. He swayed like a tree uprooted by the tempest, and fell to the ground, weeping and laughing hysterically.

"That's the way the beautiful vixen tortured the poor fellow. It was with great difficulty that I brought him to his senses.

"I wonder what good it does to Satan or Beelzebub or any other devil when human beings are plunged in such grief? What pleasure can it give to the Evil One to listen to the heartrending groans of men and women? I wonder whether the philosophers know anything about it?...

"I returned to the camp and told everything to the old men. They deliberated for some time and at last decided to wait and see how all this would turn out. And this is what happened: As we were all sitting around the camp-fire the next evening, Loyko came to us. He looked thoughtful, his features were terribly emaciated and there were black rings under his eyes which he kept fixed on the ground. Without looking at us he said: 'Listen to me, comrades. This night I have searched my heart and I no longer find in it any place for my old freedom. Radda alone now lives in it, and nothing else. Here she is, the exquisitely beautiful Radda, smiling like a queen! She loves her freedom more than she loves me, but I, I love her more than I love my freedom, and I have therefore determined to fall at her feet. Thus has she commanded me to do, in order that you might all see how her loveliness has enslaved the dauntless Loyko Zobar who, before he knew Radda, used to play with women as the vulture plays with ducks. After that, however, she will become my wife, fondling me with her kisses and embraces, so that I shall no longer have any desire to sing to you, or any regrets over the loss of my freedom! Am I right, Radda?'— Raising his eyes, he looked at her sadly. She said nothing in reply, but nodded her head vigorously and pointed at her feet. And we looked on in sorrow and amazement, not understanding it at all. We felt as though we wanted to go far away, so that we might not see Loyko Zobar falling at a woman's feet, even though this woman was Radda herself. We were overcome with a feeling of shame, pity and sorrow at this sad spectacle.

" 'Well?' said Radda to Zobar.

" 'Ah, do not be so hasty! There's plenty of time for that

yet. You will have glory enough to-day!' laughed Loyko. Like the clashing of steel—that's how his laughter sounded.

" 'Well, then, comrades, this is the whole story. What else is there left for me to do? This much. It is necessary for me to find out whether my Radda's heart is really so hard as she has shown it to be. And that's what I am going to find out now... Pardon me, my dear comrades!'

"And before we could realize what Zobar was about, Radda was already lying on the ground, and in her breast stuck Loyko's crooked knife up to its very hilt. We all stood as if paralyzed.

But Radda drew the knife out of her heart, threw it aside, pressed a lock of her black hair to the open wound, smiled and spoke up loudly and clearly: 'Farewell Loyko! I knew that you would act like this!'... And with these words on her lips she died.

"Do you understand now what kind of a girl she was, Falcon? What a woman! May I be forever cursed if she wasn't the daughter of the very devil himself! Yes, siree!

" 'And now, my proud queen, I will fall at your feet!' he cried aloud, did this Loyko, and the whole steppe reëchoed with his words. He threw himself on the ground, pressed his lips to the feet of the dead Radda, and remained as though lifeless himself. We removed our caps and surrounded the two in silence.

"What do you think of such a story, Falcon?...

"At last Nur wanted to say: 'We ought to bind him!' But not a hand would have been raised to bind Loyko Zobar, and Nur knew it. Danila, however, picked up the knife that Radda had cast aside and looked at it for a long time. His lips quivered. Radda's blood was still warm upon this knife, and it was so sharp and crooked! Then Danila approached Zobar and plunged the knife into his back, just over the heart. For he was after all the father of Radda, was this old soldier, Danila.

" 'Well done!' said Loyko in a ringing voice, turning toward Danila. And then he sank down at Radda's side and his soul followed hers out of the world.

"And there before our eyes lay Radda, her hand with its black lock of hair pressed to her bosom, her wide open eyes turned toward the sky, and at her feet lay the handsome form of Loyko Zobar. His hair had fallen over his face, and so we could not see his features.

"We stood lost in deep thought. Old Danila's gray mustache trembled and terrible was the look in his dark eyes. He gazed toward the sky, but said not a word. But the old and feeble Nur threw himself face downward on the ground and wept like a child.

"And there was good cause for weeping, Falcon! Yes, siree!...

"Well, then, God be with you, my friend. Keep going straight ahead and do not turn aside. You will only rot away if you stay in one place. That's all, Falcon!"

Makar stopped, put his pipe into his tobacco pouch and threw the folds of his cloak over his breast. The rain was drizzling, the storm increased and the surf pounded against the shore with a loud and hollow growl. One after another the horses came near the dying fire, looked at us with their big, intelligent eyes and stood around us in a big circle.

"Hop, hop, ehoi!" Makar called out to them in a friendly voice; and as he was stroking the neck of his favorite animal with the palm of his hand, he said turning to me: "It is time to sleep!" Covering his head with his cloak he stretched out on the ground and soon fell asleep. But I had no desire to sleep. I gazed through the darkness of the steppe at the roaring ocean, and I could see before me the queenly figure of the proud and lovely Radda. She held her hand with the lock of her black hair tightly pressed against her wound and through her slender brown fingers trickled the blood from her breast, drop by drop, and they fell upon the earth like ruddy stars of fire.

And behind her, close upon her heels, hovered the brave Loyko Zobar. His face was veiled by his thick black hair behind which his cold big tears flowed in a steady stream...

The rain fell faster and the wind sang a sad and solemn dirge to the proud pair—Loyko Zobar and Radda, the daughter of old Danila. And the two shadows whirled silently around each other in the darkness of the night, yet never was the singer, Loyko, able to overtake his proud, beloved Radda...

Because of Monotony

I

PUFFING voluminous volleys of thick gray smoke, the passenger-train, like an enormous reptile, disappeared in the distance of the steppe, engulfed in the yellow sea of growing corn. The rumbling of the train seemed to merge with the smoke in the hot atmosphere, and for several moments interrupted the indifferent silence of the vast, deserted plain, in the midst of which the little railroad station, because of its isolation, aroused an impression of sadness.

And when the muffled, but insistent noise of the train had grown fainter and died away under the clear dome of the cloudless sky, silence once more resumed its oppressive reign, adding to the desolate monotony of the steppe.

The steppe looked now a golden yellow; the vault of the heavens was a luminous blue; two colors of incommensurable vastness. The dark walls of the station planted in their midst produced the effect of an accidental stroke of the brush, which marred the centre of that melancholy picture, patiently painted by some artist devoid of imagination and inspiration.

Every day, at noon and at four o'clock in the afternoon there arrived at the station, on their way across the steppe, trains that stopped for four minutes. These precious minutes provided the only distraction at the station: they brought impressions to the station employees.

Each train has a multitude of distinct persons, dressed in various manners. They appear for a moment; behind the little windows of the coaches they pass rapidly by, with weary face, impatient, indifferent; the signal is given, the whistle blows, and with a nerve-wracking noise they fly off across the steppe, far away, toward the city, where men and women throng in throbbing life.

To the station employees, who are sorely bored in their solitude, it is most interesting to behold these faces; after the departure of the train they exchange impressions that have been hastily gathered. About them extends the silent steppe, above them floats the indifferent sky, and within their hearts they harbor obscure envy toward the men who every day ride by, speeding on to some unknown place, while they remain there, prisoners of the desert, as if living apart from life and in the impossibility of seeing any human countenance, except during the two hundred and forty seconds each day.

And after the train has gone they remain rooted to the platform, their eyes following the black thread that disappears in the golden sea of the prairies, silent before the manifestation of life flying past them.

They are almost all there: the chief, a corpulent red-faced personage with the mustache of a Cossack; his aide, a young fellow with reddish hair and a pointed little beard; the watchman Luka, short, inquisitive and wily, and one of the switchmen, Gomozov, a taciturn peasant, robust, with black hair, serious and full face.

Near the door of the station, seated on a bench, is the chief's wife, a fat little woman who suffers much from the heat; in her lap slumbers an infant with cheeks as bulging and as red as his mother's.

The locomotive and the coaches disappear behind a slope, as if the train had been swallowed by the earth.

Then the chief turns to his wife and says:

"Well Sofia! Is the samovar ready?"

"It certainly is," she replies sweetly, with a languid voice.

"Luka! Hey there! Sweep the road. Can't you see they've filled it with all kinds of filth?"

"Yes, I know, Matvei Yegorovitch."

"Very well. Shall we have tea, Nikolai Petrovitch?"

"So as not to break the custom," replies the aide.

And when the four o'clock train has left, Matvei Yegorovitch says to his wife:

"Well Sofia! Is dinner ready?"

Then he gives the order to Luka, — always the same order, and invites his aide who dines with them.

"Good. . . . Shall we eat?"

And his aide replies, properly:

"As always."

They walk from the platform to the dining-room, where there are many flowers and few pieces of furniture, — where the odor of the kitchen is perceptible, as well as that of the infant's swaddling-clothes, and there, seated around the table, they speak of what speeds by the station.

"Did you notice, Nikolai Petrovitch, a brunette dressed in yellow who was in one of the second-class coaches? There was a stunning beauty for you!"

"Not at all bad, but dressed without taste," answered the aide.

He always spoke in a curt, sententious manner, for he believed himself to be an educated man, conversant with life. He had been to college. In a little note-book bound in black cloth he was wont to inscribe sayings of famous men, phrases culled from the feuilletons of newspapers and from the books that came by accident into his hands. The chief never contradicted him; in all matters that did not concern the service he listened attentively to his adjutant. The wise aphorisms from Nikolai Petrovitch's note-book pleased him especially, and he was frank in his admiration of them. The aide's "but" in regard to the brunette evoked a query from Matvei Yegorovitch.

"Then you don't think that yellow becomes brunettes?"

"I refer to her manner, not the color," explained Nikolai

Petrovitch, carefully taking some preserves which he brought forth from a crystal jar to place in the dessert plate.

"Manner is a thing by itself," admitted the chief.

His wife joined in the discussion, for such a subject was within her scope and of direct concern to her.

But since the minds of such persons are very little exercised the conversation proceeds slowly, rarely penetrating to their feelings.

And through the window the silent steppe gazes in upon them, and the sky, majestic in its proud serenity.

At every moment freight trains arrive, but the personnel of these trains has been known to them for a long time. They are all half-asleep fellows, oppressed by the monotony of the journeys across the steppe. Of course sometimes they relate an accident that occurred on the line. But news of this character arouses no reflection: it is devoured just as epicures swallow a rare and savory dish.

And the sun slowly descends in the heavens, until it reaches the edge of the steppe, and when it has almost touched the earth it turns purple. A red tint covers the plain, which awakes an apprehensive mood of insufficiency, a vague aspiration towards something far away, beyond that emptiness. The rim of the sun then touches the earth. For a long time after its disappearance there sounds in the sky the music of the sunset's resplendent colors, and twilight arrives, warm and silent. The stars light up and tremble in the heavens, as if terrified by the monotony that reigns on earth.

With the coming of twilight the steppe grows smaller; the darknesses of dusk arise from all directions and make for the station, and night falls, black and lugubrious.

The station lamps are lighted; brighter and higher than the others is the light of the signal-desk. Around it, darkness and silence.

At each instant there is the sound of a bell: a signal that

a train is approaching; the funeral tolling of the bell crosses the steppe, where it is quickly extinguished.

A short while after the ringing, a vivid light draws nearer, and the silence of the steppe trembles with the muffled noise of the train, which rolls toward the solitary station, surrounded by darkness.

II

The lower stratum of the society of the station maintains a life somewhat distinct from that of the aristocracy. The watchman Luka struggles perpetually with his desire to run off to his wife and his brother, who live in the town, seven versts away. That's where his home is, as he says to Gomozov when he orders the taciturn, leisurely switchman to lend a helping hand in the station.

At the word "home" Gomozov always sighs heavily and says to Luka:

"Yes, you're right. . . One's home requires care. . . .

And the other switchman, Afanassi Yagodka, an old soldier with a round, ruddy face encircled by gray hairs, and of jesting, malicious propensities, refuses to believe Luka.

"Home!" he exclaims mockingly. "His wife! I know very well what that means. . . . Is your wife a widow? Or perhaps some soldier's spouse?"

"Shut up, you king of the fowl!" retorts Luka, scornfully.

He dubs Yagodka king of the fowl because the old soldier professes a deep affection for birds. His entire house is covered, inside as well as outside, with cages and dove-cotes; within and without, all day long is heard the ceaseless trilling and cooing of the birds. Imprisoned by the soldier the quails sing their monotonous "pay your debts," the starlings murmur long discourses, many-colored birds whisper tirelessly, whistle or trill, enlivening the soldier's sombre existence. Taking care of them during the time left free to him by his work, he treats them with the utmost tenderness and solicitude, not interesting himself at all in his companions.

Luka he calls a snake, — Gomozov a katsap,* and openly terms them "women chasers," saying that they should be whipped for it.

Luka gives little heed to his words; but if the soldier succeeds in rousing his anger, for a long time he grumbles in most offensive manner.

"Gray barracks beast! Garrison rat! What can you understand? You spent your whole life chasing the frogs behind the cannons. Who's telling you to say anything? Back to your partridges, — command them, order your fowl about!"

Yagodka, after having heard the watchman's insults, calmly went to lodge complaint with the chief, who shouted that he didn't want people coming to him and pestering him with nonsense, and dismissed the soldier unceremoniously. Whereupon the soldier betook himself to Luka and in his turn insulted him without getting excited about it, calmly, with execrable words full of meaning, until Luka dashed off, leaving him alone.

"What can you do? There's no getting along with that fellow! No doubt it's all silly; just the same, 'Judge not that ye be not judged. . . .' "

On a certain occasion the soldier answered him with a loud guffaw.

"Poll-parrot! 'Judge not, judge not. . . .' why, if people didn't judge one another they'd have nothing to talk about."

Besides the chief's wife there was another woman in the station, — the cook. Her name was Arina; she was almost forty, and very ugly: obese, with hanging breasts, always dirty and ragged. She waddled like a duck, and in her freckled face beamed two little darting eyes surrounded by a network of wrinkles. There was something submissive, oppressed, about her ill-formed person, and her fleshy lips curled out constantly,

* Name given by inhabitants of Great Russia to those of Little Russia.

as if she wanted to implore pardon of all men, throw herself at their feet, yet not daring to cry. Gomozov spent eight months in the station without paying any special heed to the cook; whenever he met her he would simply wish her "good day!" She would reply in like manner, they would exchange two or three sentences and would continue on their way. But one day Gomozov came to the chief's kitchen to ask Arina to mend a few of his shirts. The cook consented, and after they were mended, for some reason or other, she brought them to Gomozov in person.

"Ah! A thousand thanks!" he said. "Three shirts at ten kopeks apiece makes thirty kopeks I owe you,— correct?"

"Correct," replied Arina.

Gomozov sank into a revery and was silent for some time.

"What district do you come from?" he finally asked the woman, who, while he was mediating had scrutinized his beard.

"From Riazan," she answered.

"That's very far! And how do you come here?"

"Why, to tell the truth, ... I'm alone .... all alone—"

"That can carry one farther still," sighed Gomozov.

There followed a long silence.

"What a coincidence! I, too, am alone. I come from the district of Sergatch," Gomozov began to say. "I, too am alone .... all alone. I once had a wife. ... a child, two children. ... My wife died during an epidemic of cholera, and the children. .. from something or other, perhaps because their last hour had come. ... died, too. And I, ... how shall I say? I was left without a compass to guide me. ... Misfortune. ... Yes, after that I tried without success to establish myself once more. But the machine had fallen apart; it no longer worked and I began to go, as one would say, out of my path. ... And here it is three years that I've dragged along in my wretchedness."

"It's bad not to have a husband!" murmured Arina sweetly.

"I should think so. You are a widow, perhaps?"

"Unmarried."

"You don't say!" exclaimed Gomozov incredulously.

"Upon my word!" affirmed Arina.

"How is it you never married?"

"Who was going to take me? I've nothing . . . . how could I tempt anyone? If I'd have been good-looking at least!"

"Yes," slowly uttered Gomozov, who had remained meditating.

And stroking his beard he began to examine her with penetrating glance. . . . Then he inquired what wages she received.

"Two fifty."

"Good. There are thirty kopeks coming to you? Listen to what I say to you. Come for them tonight. . . . around ten o'clock. What do you say? I'll give them to you then, we'll have tea, and we'll dance to drive away the monotony. . . . We're both so lonesome. . . . Come, won't you?"

"I'll come," she promised, impatiently.

And she left.

Later, having returned to the house punctually at ten o'clock, she departed from Gomozov at dawn.

He did not repeat his invitation, nor did he give her the thirty kopeks.

Arina came again of her own accord, meek and submissive, and silently planted herself before him. He, stretched out upon the bed, gazed at her and rolling toward the wall, said, "Sit down."

When she had sat down he admonished her:

"Hear what I tell you. . . . Keep this secret. Let nobody know! . . . . Understand? Otherwise things would be very unpleasant. . . . I'm no youngster, nor are you, either. . . . Understand?"

She nodded affirmatively.

When they parted he gave her some clothes that needed mending and warned her again:

"Nobody! Not a soul!"

And thus they lived, hiding their relations from everybody.

Arina came to his house in spite of all, almost dragging herself. He received her with great condescension, affecting lordly airs, and at times he would say to her, frankly:

"How ugly you are!"

She would smile in silence, — an insipid, guilty smile, and when she left him she would take along something to repair.

They did not meet often. But on various occasions, encountering her at the station, he would say to her in a low voice:

"Come tonight."

And Arina would go meekly, with a serious expression on her freckled face, as if she were intent upon fulfilling an important duty.

And when she returned to the station her countenance would wear its habitual lugubrious expression of guilt and fright.

At times she would stop at some nook sheltered by a tree of the steppe. Here reigned night, and in the austere silence her heart would compress with fear.

III

On a certain occasion, after having seen the four o'clock train leave, the higher employees of the station organized a tea-party in the garden, before the windows of Matvei Yegorovitch's rooms, in the leafy shade of the poplars.

It was a hot-weather custom that introduced a touch of variety into the monotony of their existence.

They would sip tea and look at each other in silence after having exhausted all the subjects suggested by the train.

"It's even hotter today than yesterday," commented Matvei Yegorovitch, handing his wife the jar and with the other hand wiping the perspiration that bedewed his forehead.

The woman took the jar and observed:

"It simply seems hotter because of the monotony."

"H'm! .... Perhaps. . . . Really.... How tedious existence is! Now cards, for example, are good in cases like this.... But we are only three...."

Nikolai Petrovitch shrugged his shoulders, blinked, and announced, in a clear voice:

"Cards, according to Schopenhauer, are the bankruptcy of intellect."

"Well expressed!" enthused Matvei Yegorovitch. "Very well. 'The bankruptcy of intellect'. . . . Yes. And who said that?"

"Schopenhauer, a German philosopher. . . ."

"A philosopher! So-o!"

"And tell me. These philosophers. . . . Are they, maybe, employees of the Universities?" asked Sofia Ivanovna.

"It is. . . . how shall I explain it? . . . . it's not a position but.... so to say, a natural gift.... Everybody can be a philosopher.... Everyone who's born with the habit of thinking about the beginning and the end of things. Of course, there are philosophers in the universities, but you can be one anywhere at all.... even if you happen to be an employee at a railroad station."

"And do those in the universities see very much?"

"That depends on their.... intelligence."

"But if there were only one more we could have started a fine game!" sighed Matvei Yegorovitch.

And the conversation languished.

The larks sing in the blue heavens, the linnets flit from branch to branch of the poplars, chirping sweetly. Inside a child is crying.

"Is Arina there?" asked Matvei Yegorovitch.

"Certainly," replied his wife in a low voice.

"A queer creature," observed Nikolai Petrovitch.

"Eccentricity is the first manifestation of triviality," remarked Nikolai Petrovitch sententiously, with a dreamy, meditative air.

"How's that?" asked the chief, interested.

And Nikolai Petrovitch, repeating the aphorism with a professorial air, rolls his eyes in a voluptuous manner, while Sofia Ivanovna says, in a languid little voice:

"How well you remember what you've read! And here I can't recall what I read yesterday!"

"Habit," replied Nikolai Petrovitch curtly.

"No, that other fellow is better. What do you call him? Schopenhauer?" said Matvei Yegorovitch with a smile. "So that whatever is young will become old."

"And vice versa, for a poet has written: 'All that is new comes from what has been left by the old.'"

"The devil! How can you remember all that? It gushes from you like water from a fountain!"

Matvei Yegorovitch laughed contentedly; his wife smiled with a kindly air, and Nikolai Petrovitch tried in vain to hide his pleasure at the compliment.

"And who said that about triviality?"

"Bariatinsky, a poet."

"And that other quotation?"

"Fofanov, another poet."

"There's a couple of smart fellows for you!" enthused Matvei Yegorovitch.

"And with a musical voice, laughing with contentment, he repeated the two citations.

It seems that monotony plays with them. For a moment it frees them from its clutches, then once more grasps them in its power. Then they become silent, suffering from the heat, which is increased by the tea.

In the station, only silence; on the steppe, only the sun.

"Oh, yes! I was about to speak of Arina!" recalls Matvei Yegorovitch. "There's a strange woman for you! I watch her with wonder. As if she were crushed by something. She doesn't laugh, or sing, and speaks very little. . . . You'd think she was a piece of wood! And yet she's a wonderful worker, and she's so careful with Lelia, so devoted to the child. . . ."

He speaks in a low voice, but wishes nevertheless that Arina will hear him through the window. He knows that servants swell with pride upon hearing themselves praised. His wife interrupts him with a meaningful rebuke.

"None of that. You don't know much about her."

Whereupon Nikolai Petrovitch, beating time with a spoon on the table, began to murmur sweetly, as if declaiming:

> A slave am I of love,
> And deep is my despair,
> When in the lists I enter,
> 'Gainst you, my demon fair!

He smiled.

"How now? What's that you're saying? She. . . . Ah, you've got something between you!"

And Matvei Yegorovitch laughed heartily. His cheeks shook and beads of perspiration rolled down his forehead.

"There's nothing so wonderful about her," said his wife. "In the first place, she doesn't take good care of the child. In the second, have you noticed the kind of bread she makes? Bitter, burned. And why?"

"Yes, indeed. There is something the matter with the bread. . . . We'll have to speak to her about it. But, the deuce! I didn't expect anything like this! So she's a regular heart-breaker? Devil take me! And who's the man? Lukachka? I'll tease the life out of the old devil! Yagodka? The toothless dandy!"

"Gomozov," said Nikolai Petrovitch curtly.

"So grave a fellow as that! O-oh! But you're. . . . You're not fooling, are you?"

Such a shocking bit of gossip amused Matvei Yegorovitch

immensely. He was soon laughing in loud outbursts, tears coming to his eyes; first he spoke of the necessity of giving the lovers a severe reprimand; then he began to imagine the tender conversations that passed between them, and exploded anew in a deafening roar.

At last he became petulant. Nikolai Petrovitch assumed a serious face, while Sofia Ivanovna brusquely interrupted her husband's talk.

"The devil! I don't have to pay his debts, do I? This is interesting!" continued Matvei Yegorovitch, unable to control himself.

At this juncture Luka appeared, saying, not very correctly, "The telegraph is calling."

"I'm going. Give the signal to 42."

In another moment he was beside the aide at the station. where Luka replied to the telegraph call. Nikolai Petrovitch went to the apparatus and asked the next station, "Can I send train 42?"

The chief passed through the office, smiled and said, "We've got to play those devils a trick. Just to kill time and conquer this deadly monotony.... We may well be permitted to laugh for once."

"Certainly, that's permissible," agreed Nikolai Petrovitch, without leaving the apparatus.

For he knew that philosophy must be expressed in a laconic manner.

IV

The opportunity for indulging in a little laughter was not slow in presenting itself.

On a certain night Gomozov went to the shack where Arina, by his order and with permission of her master had arranged a bed amid all the old furniture. The place was exposed and damp, and the broken boxes, the casks, the tables and all the other objects assumed in the darkness the most terrifying shapes. When Arina was alone in the midst of all this she was so afraid that she could scarcely sleep, and she recited all the prayers she had ever learned, in a subdued voice.

Gomozov came, and for a long time silently took her to him, and after he had become tired he fell asleep. But he was soon awakened by the uneasy whispering of Arina.

"Timofei Petrovitch. Timofei Petrovitch!"

"What's the matter?" asked Gomozov, not yet thoroughly awake.

"We've been locked in!"

"What do you mean?" he exclaimed, sitting up with a start.

"Somebody came here and with some chains. . . ."

"Are you crazy?" he grumbled, angrily and in terror, thrusting her from him.

Gomozov arose, and stumbling against several objects made his way to the door, pushed it, and after a silence said, ill-humoredly, "The soldier!"

Someone on the other side of the door laughed gleefully.

"Open!" begged Gomozov aloud.

"What's that?"

It was the soldier's voice.

"I tell you to open!"

"Tomorrow morning," replied the soldier.

And he went off.

"I've got to get to work!" cried Gomozov, in tones of mingled anger and entreaty.

"I'll attend to your duties. Don't worry."

"You dog, you!" murmured the switchman, in anxiety "Wait a while! You haven't any right to lock me up. . . . He has the key. . . . What'll you tell him? He'll ask, 'Where is Gomozov?' And. . . . Ha?. . . . Answer him!"

"But, you must know that the order for this came from the chief himself," said Arina in a low, despairing voice.

"The chief?" stammered Gomozov, horrified. "Why?"

And then, after a moment's silence.

"You lie!" he exclaimed.

She replied with a deep sigh.

"What will this lead to?" wondered the switchman, sitting down upon something near the door. What a disgrace for me! And all on account of you, you ugly old witch!"

With his fists doubled up Gomozov made a threatening gesture toward the direction whence came the breathing. She, on her side, was careful not to say a word.

A dark dampness surrounded them, a darkness impregnated with the odor of limestone, mould, and something acrid that seemed to pierce the nostrils. Strips of moonlight came through the cracks of the door. Behind, a freight train leaving the station rumbled off noisily.

"What good is this silence?" asked Gomozov, in a rage. "What am I to do now? First you commit follies and then you're silent? Think, devil take you! What are we to do? Where can I hide to conceal this shame? Oh, good Lord in heaven! Why did I ever fall in with such a. . . ."

"I'll implore pardon," said Arina, in a low voice.

"And then?"

"Perhaps they'll forgive. . . ."

"What good will that do me? If they pardon you! Well, what then? On whom will the disgrace fall? It's me that they'll laugh at!"

After another pause he began to curse her anew. And the time passed with cruel slowness. At last the woman, in a trembling voice, said to him, entreatingly, "Timofei Petrovitch, forgive me!"

"You ought to be forgiven with a good rap on the head!" he snarled.

Again a long silence, lugubrious, unnerving, full of suffering and suppressed anger for the two persons imprisoned in the darkness.

"Good heavens! If only day would come more quickly!" wailed Arina in her perplexity.

"Shut up, or I'll knock daylight into you!" scowled Gomozov, returning to his bitter reproaches.

And once again the torture of silence fell over them. And the cruelty of time increased with the approach of day, as if each minute retarded its progress, maliciously enjoying the ludicrous, yet grievous situation of the two persons.

At last Gomozov fell asleep, but the song of a rooster, crowing near the cabin, awoke him.

"Hey there, witch! Are you sleeping?" he asked, in a muffled voice.

"No," answered Arina, with a deep sigh.

"Wouldn't you like a nice little nap?" proposed the switchman, ironically. "Come. . . ."

"Timofei Petrovitch!" implored Arina with a shrill cry. "Don't torment me! Have pity on me! In the name of Christ, son of God, have pity on me! I'm alone, all alone! And you, my beloved. . . ."

"None of your howling, and don't make yourself ridiculous," interjected Gomozov seriously, quieting the hysteric muttering of the woman, who had moved him somewhat. "Hush! When the Lord begins to punish. . . ."

And anew they waited in silence for the passing of each minute. But the moments went by without bringing anything. At last, through the cracks of the door could be seen the gleam of the sun's rays, which illuminated the darkness of the cabin. Somebody came to the door, listened for a moment and then went away.

"Hangman!" growled Gomozov.

And he spat out.

Another period of waiting, silent and tyrannical.

"Good Lord, I beg You!" murmured Arina.

It seemed that someone was slowly coming near. The chain rattled, and the voice of the chief was heard.

"Gomozov! Take Arina by the hand and come out! At once!"

"Come," said Gomozov to her, in a low voice.

Arina, with bowed head, came over to his side.

The door was opened; the chief appeared. He saluted and said, "My congratulations to the young couple! Forward! Strike up the band!"

Gomozov passed the threshold and came to a sudden halt, stupefied by a wild, confused tumult. Behind the door were Luka, Yagodka and Nikolai Petrovitch.

Luka was beating his fist against a pail, howling something in a quivering tenor voice; the soldier was blowing his bagpipe, and Matvei Yegorovitch was making wild gestures, his cheeks puffed out, and making a trumpet-like sound through his lips.

Pum, pum! Pum-pum-pum!

The pail thumped, the bagpipe wheezed and groaned, and Matvei Yegorovitch laughed madly. His aide, too, exploded with laughter when he beheld Gomozov in utter confusion, with a sinister face and silly laugh upon his trembling lips. Behind him was Arina, half petrified, her head bowed low upon her breast.

"Arina, to her lover,
Spoke very tender words."

Luka sang, making terrible gestures in Gomozov's direction.

And the soldier approached. Placing his bagpipe next to the switchman's ear he played on and on.

"Excellent. Now proceed, proceed. Arm in arm!" cried the chief.

His wife was seated in the vestibule, and she swayed from side to side, uttering penetrating shrieks.

"Motria, enough. Oh, I'll die of laughing!"

> Who, for a taste of the beauty's lips,
> Wouldn't brave the stoutest whips?

It was the aide who sang, almost into Gomozov's ear.

"Long live the young couple!" shouted Matvei Yegorovitch as Gomozov took a step forward.

And from the throats of all rose a unanimous hurrah, the soldier shouting with a roaring bass.

Arina walked behind Gomozov with raised head, her mouth open, her arms hanging at her side. Her eyes peered vaguely forward, but it is doubtful whether they saw anything.

"Motria, order them to embrace.... Ha, ha, ha!"

"Bride and bridegroom, this is bitter!" shouted Nikolai Petrovitch, using the phrase employed at the embracing of a newly-wed pair.

And Matvei Yegorovitch leaned against a tree, for he was so weak from laughing that his feet shook beneath him.

And the pail kept dinning away, while the bagpipe wheezed and groaned, and Luka danced as he sang:

> "Oh, lovely cook Arina,
> You've made us a pretty thick soup."

And Nikolai Petrovitch began once more to trumpet through his lips, "Pum, pum, pum! Tra, ta, ta! Pum, pum! Tra, ta, ta!"

Gomozov went as far as the door of a certain shanty and suddenly made his escape through it. Arina was left in the yard surrounded by her almost delirious persecutors. They shouted, laughed, whistled into her ears and jumped about her in a paroxysm of crazy joy.

Arina stood before them with impassive countenance, dirty, pitiful, ridiculous.

"The young bridegroom has gone off, and she.... remains here," shouted Matvei Yegorovitch to his wife, pointing to Arina and bursting anew into loud guffaws.

Arina turned her head toward him, walked by the cabin, and suddenly fled to the steppe. She was followed by a din of whistling, shouts and laughter.

"Enough! Let her alone!" shouted Sofia Ivanovna. "Let her get back her courage. She has to make dinner for us soon."

Arina went further and further into the steppe, yonder where, behind the land used for the railroad there arose the bristling fringes of the corn. She walked slowly, like one absorbed in her thoughts.

"What's that you say?" asked Matvei Yegorovitch of the various actors in the farce, who were recounting to each other the most trivial details of the event.

And everybody laughed. Even Nikolai Petrovitch found an aphorism for the occasion.

"In truth it is no sin
To laugh at the ridiculous."

he said to Sofia Ivanovna.

And then he added, with an air of importance, "But to laugh excessively is unhealthy."

Despite this, there was a great deal of laughter in the station that day; but it didn't go so well with the eating, for, since Arina had not returned, the chief's wife had to do the cooking. Yet even the tasteless meal was not enough to extinguish the good humor of the group. Gomozov did not fare forth from the cabin until his duties called him, and when he came out he was summoned to the chief's office, where Nikolai Petrovitch, much to Matvei Yegorovitch's delight, asked him how he had succeeded in seducing his beauty.

"For its originality it is a sin of the first class," said Nikolai Petrovitch to the chief.

"It certainly is," assented the composed switchman with a forced laugh.

For he had suddenly begun to understand that by telling

the story in a manner to cast ridicule upon Arina he himself would be less laughed at.

And he began:

"At first we made eyes at each other. . . ."

"Made eyes at each other? Ha, ha, ha! Just imagine, Nikolai Petrovitch, how an ugly thing like that would make eyes! This is delicious!"

"Well, but she did make them at me. And when I saw that, I said to myself, 'You can have a little amusement!' Then she asked me, 'Do you want me to sew your shirts?'"

"But the subtlety of the phrase was not in the sewing," observed Nikolai Petrovitch.

And he explained to the chief.

"That, you know, is from Nekrassov. Continue, Timofei."

And Timofei continued his explanations; at first he forced himself, then gradually he began to believe his own lie, for he saw that his lie was useful.

V

And meanwhile, she of whom he spoke was stretched out in the steppe. She had made her way into the depths of the sea of corn, and had dropped upon the earth, where she remained for a long time motionless. When the hot sun began to burn her shoulder until she could stand it no longer, she turned over with her mouth facing the sky, covering her face with her hands, so that her eyes should not see the heavens, which were too clear, nor the sun, which was too bright.

Under the breath of the wind the corn produced a weak noise about that woman crushed with shame, and the countless crickets chirped tirelessly, as if intent upon very important business. And it was hot. The woman tried to recall her prayers, but she could not. Before her eyes there swayed in a wild dance faces contracted with laughter, while in her ears boomed the tenor voice of Luka and the mocking, querelous notes of the bagpipe, and the resounding shouts. Either this, or the heat, oppressed her bosom; she tore open her chemise, exposed her skin to the rays of the sun, hoping, perhaps, that in this way she might breathe more comfortably. And while the sun toasted her skin, a strange sensation burrowed about within her breast. With deep sighs, from time to time she murmured, "Good God, I entreat You!"

But the only response that came to her ears was the dry rustling of the corn and the chirping of the crickets. When she raised her head above the waves of the corn she beheld its golden reflection, the black chimney of the water-house that rose behind the station in the little valley, and the roof of the house in which they were all laughing at her plight. There was nothing else in the boundless yellow plain, covered by the blue dome of heaven, and to Arina it seemed that she was all alone in the world, — that she was stretched out exactly in its centre, and that there was none who would offer to share with her the burden of solitude.

At night she heard cries.

"Arina! Arina, — the devil!"

One of the voices she recognized as Luka's, — the other was the soldier. She would have liked to hear a certain other voice, but that one was not heard; then she began to weep copiously. The tears ran down her cheeks and on to her bosom. She wept, and as she wept she rubbed her naked skin against the earth, so as not to feel the inner burning that tormented her more and more. She cried, then tried to stop, stifling her groans, as if afraid that someone would hear her and forbid her to cry.

Afterward, when night had come, she arose and walked slowly toward the station.

Arrived there she leaned against the wall of the shack, and there she remained a long time, her gaze fixed upon the steppe. She could make out a freight train and she heard the soldier relating the story of her shame, and heard the laughter of the conductors.

The night was peaceful, a moonlit night. . . . The loud guffaws echoed afar, across the desolate steppe, where the sound of the locomotive's whistle died away.

"Good Lord, I beg You!" sighed the woman, leaning more heavily against the wall.

But her sighs did not lighten the burden that she felt upon her heart.

VI

The next morning she made her way into the attic of the station and hanged herself, using a rope that formerly had served for putting out clothes to dry.

Two days later, on account of the odor of the body, the corpse was discovered. At first they were afraid, then they began to inquire as to who was to blame. Nikolai Petrovitch demonstrated conclusively that it was Gomozov's fault. The chief then struck Gomozov with his closed fist and ordered the switchman to shut up.

The authorities began to investigate. As a result they found that Arina used to suffer from attacks of melancholy. . . . The laborers about the station were ordered to bury the corpse in the steppe. And when this had been carried out, order and quiet returned to the station.

And its inhabitants began to live their four minutes per day, dying of monotony and solitude, of idleness and the heat. With envious glances they followed the trains that sped past them.

And in winter, when the tempests, in a wild charge, loosen their fury upon the steppe, and boom their wailings, and envelop the station in snow and wild shrieks, the life of its denizens becomes more monotonous than ever.

The Man Who Could Not Die

(From "Old Isergil")

IT was in Dobrudja, at the mouth of the Danube, that old Isergil told me the story which I am relating here.

One evening, when the grape-gathering was over for the day, the Maldavians employed in the vineyard went to the seashore, but I remained alone with old Isergil. We lay on the ground in the thick shade of the vines, observing silently the gradually disappearing outlines of the people as they seemed more and more to melt into the gathering darkness.

They were laughing and singing as they strolled along: the men — sunburnt and sturdy, with long black mustache and thick shocks of hair that fell over their shoulders, their stalwart forms dressed in short jackets and wide trousers; the women and the girls — gay, pretty and supple as willow twigs, with dark blue eyes and tanned faces whose black and silk-soft hair fastened with garlands of coins, played loosely in the warm and wanton breeze. The bells tinkled softly as the wind swept over the wide steppe. Now and then, when a sudden puff rushed through the darkness as though in combat with an invisible force, their hair was blown high over their heads in fantastic shapes. Seen from a distance, these shapes gave to the gradually vanishing women a wonderful, fairy-like appearance. Farther they went and farther, and the magic of the darkness threw about them a mantle that seemed more and more wonderfully fantastic.

Now arose the sound of a violin, a girl sang in a velvety alto voice, and laughter came to our ears. And the imagination, having burst the bonds of reality in the bewitching twilight, wove all these sounds into a wreath of gaily-colored ribbons and flowers of melody which hovered gracefully over the dim outlines of the toilers.

The evening air was becoming permeated with the sharp salty tang of the sea, mingled with the warm, pungent odor of the rain-soaked earth. A few clouds that seemed to have been torn away from the recent rain-storm, still straggled in the air, curling softly and tinting with luxurious colors the western sky, — now white and feathery, now steel-gray, now, towering like sun-drenched cliffs, golden and rosy and red, and now black and threatening. And through these clouds, fragments of blue sky, already glittering with innumerable stars, peeped tenderly over the steppe. All this, — the perfume, the clouds, the stars and the people — shone with a bewitching beauty in the fragrant golden twilight; and yet an atmosphere of indescribable sadness hovered over everything, as at the beginning of a fairy tale. Everything was alive, harmoniously and beautifully alive, and yet the hand of death seemed to be over all, as though their luxuriant growth were suddenly arrested. This life lacked the nervous action of real life; it lacked those sounds which have the power of latent growth. The sounds that reached the ear at this time, however, were faint and broken, and as they were dying away they seemed to be transformed into soft sighs, — sighs of regret and of longing. Longing for what? Happiness, perhaps, — that elusive, unrecognizable will-o'-the-wisp, human happiness? . . . .

As these tones floated through the air I was filled with fanciful desires. I wished that I might be tranformed into dust and that I might be blown by the wind in every direction. I longed to flow like a warm stream through the steppe, to sweep into the sea and to rise in soft vapor amongst the beautiful clouds. I wished that I, and I alone, could permeate that entire sorrowful, magical night. And I became melancholy without myself knowing the reason why.

"Why haven't you gone with the others?" asked old Isergil as she nodded toward the sea.

She was bent with old age, almost doubled like a half-closed jack-knife. Her once dark blue eyes were sad and tearful. Her voice sounded dry and thin, without the slightest vibration. Her words seemed to issue from her creaking bones. It was a miracle that she could still speak at all!

"I didn't care to," I replied.

"Well, well, well! You are born old, you people of the North. You are as sullen as the very devil. Our girls are afraid of you, and yet you are so young and strong."

The moon had risen. Its orb was big and blood-red. It seemed to have been born out of the womb of the steppe which had grown fat and fertile through the centuries with the flesh and the blood of numberless human victims swallowed therein. The shadows of the vine leaves wove delicate lace patterns around us, covering us as with a net whose meshes danced and trembled without end. And to the left of us quivered the shadows of the clouds, bright and transparent in the shimmering moonbeams. We could just barely hear the murmur of the sea in the distance, the soft weeping of the violin, the cheerful laughter of a young girl, the vibrant baritone of her companion, — all harmonizing with the regular lilt and ripple of the waves against the shore.

"Look! There comes Larra!"

I followed with my eyes the crooked finger of old Isergil and I saw quivering shadows, many shadows, — and one of them, darker and thicker, hovered lower and faster than the rest. It was the shadow of a layer of clouds that moved over the sky faster and lower than the clouds directly overhead.

"I see nobody there," I said.

Why, you are blinder than I, old woman though I am. Look,

there — don't you see? That black thing that flies so fast over the steppe."

I looked again, and once more I saw nothing but shadows.

"That is nothing but a shadow," I said. "Why do you call it Larra?"

"Because it is Larra! He has turned into a mere shadow. And it is time he did! He has been living for thousands of years already, and the sun has sucked out all his blood and marrow and the wind has shrivelled up his body. Thus does God punish human beings for their overweening pride!"

"Tell me about it," I begged of the old gipsy, already picturing to myself one of those exquisite fairy tales the like of which you can hear only in the steppe.

And old Isergil began her story:

"It happened many thousands of years ago. Far over the sea, toward the rising of the sun lies the land of the Great Stream, and in that land every leaf on every tree and every blade of grass gives out just as much shade as a man needs in order to shield himself against the sun, which shines there with a terrible blaze. So generous is the earth in that country!

"Once upon a time there lived in that land a race of mighty men who tended their herds and spent their days in hunting wild beasts. At the end of every hunt they regaled themselves with merry feasts, singing songs and making love to the girls who were flame-bright in their loveliness in that land.

"Once, in the midst of their banquet, an eagle swooped down from the sky and carried off one of their maidens. Dark was her hair and her body was tender and fragrant as the night. The arrows which the men shot after the eagle fell back to earth. They looked for the maiden everywhere, but they could not find her. And in time she was forgotten, just as everything else is forgotten."

The old gipsy sighed and then became silent. Her creaking

voice sounded like the jarring of the forgotten centuries stirred into life again and awaking within her breast the shadow of a memory. And the sea accompanied harmoniously the beginning of this old, old legend, one of the many that had their birth in the gray dawn of the world where the wind of the land and the waves of the ocean whispered together.

"Twenty years later the maiden returned, shattered and weary, and with her came a youth, strong and handsome as she herself had once been. And when they asked her where she had lived all this time she told them how the eagle had carried her off to his nest among the mountains where she dwelt as his wife. The youth was his son, but the father was no longer alive; for that mighty eagle, when he felt that he was growing feeble and old and that his end was approaching, raised himself with a final effort on high toward the sun, folded his wings and allowed himself to be dashed to pieces on the jagged rocks below.

"Everybody looked in amazement at the eagle's son and they noticed that he was in no way different from them except that his eye was proud and cold and invincible as the eye of the monarch of the air. When they spoke to him, he replied or kept silent, just as he pleased; and when the elders addressed him, he answered them as though he were their equal. This displeased them, and they called him an unfinished arrow whose barb had been left unsharpened, and they explained that many thousands of people like himself and even much older than himself honored and obeyed them. But he looked at them with his cold haughty eyes, remarking that there was not another man in the world like himself. If others honored and obeyed the elders, it was their affair; but as for him, it was his intention not to abide by the elders' wishes.

"Hereupon they became enraged and cried out that there was no place for him in their midst! 'Let him go wherever he wishes!' they said. He laughed and went wherever he wished, — namely, to a beautiful young girl who had been looking at him long and steadily. He approached her and took her in his arms. This girl, however, was the daughter of one of the elders who had just rebuked him. And although he was handsome, she spurned his embrace, for she feared the wrath of her father. She pushed him away from her and was about to leave, but he followed her; and as she fell down, he placed his foot upon her breast. He crushed it so fiercely that the blood began to spurt out of her mouth and her life rushed forth from her writhing heart.

"All those who had witnessed this were overwhelmed with terror, for never had they beheld a human being slain in such a manner. And for a long time they were silent, gazing at the dead maiden as she lay there with her terrified, distended eyes and bleeding mouth that even in death seemed dumbly crying for revenge. And they gazed at him as he stood there alone, cold and defiant, with his head raised high, inviting the punishment that he knew would fall upon his head. Finally, recovering their senses, they seized and bound him, and then left him there; for they thought it too merciful a punishment to put him to death at once for such a horrible and unheard-of crime as he had committed."

The darkness of the night was spreading, its meshes interwoven with the soft threads of melody still heard in the distance, its tints becoming more and more fantastic. The crickets chirrupped among the trembling vine leaves, the winds sighed and whispered to one another, and the full moon, blood-red hitherto, gradually grew more silvery, scattering its shimmer lavishly over the wide steppe.

"And they gathered together to determine upon the penalty that might be worthy of his crime. One of them proposed to have him torn asunder by two horses pulling in opposite directions. This, however, did not satisfy them. Another one suggested that they should all shoot their arrows at him. But this, too, did not seem punishment enough. Some recommended that they should burn him at the stake; but in that case the smoke would hide his suffering from their eyes. They discussed this thing and that thing, but they found no torture that satisfied them all. And his mother knelt before the elders, but found neither words nor tears to soften their hearts with pity toward her son. For a long time they deliberated, until finally a wise man said: 'Let us ask him why he did it!'

"They asked him and he replied: 'First remove my chains. Unless I am freed I refuse to talk to you!'

"And when they had removed his chains he said: 'What do you want?' And he asked this in the tone of a master speaking to his slaves.

" 'You have already heard what we want,' replied the wise man.

" 'Why should I explain my actions to you?'

" 'In order that we may understand you, O terrible eagle! Now listen to us. Your life is forfeited anyhow, so that you had better tell us why you have killed her. We are going to live on and it is necessary that we should learn more than we already know.'

" 'Very well, I will tell you, although I myself do not know just what has happened. It seems to me that I killed her because she spurned me when I desired to embrace her.'

" 'But she was not yours!'

" 'Do you use only that which is yours? I think that each man brings with him nothing but his speech, his hands and his feet. These alone are his by right of birth. And yet do not all of you possess wives, beasts of burden, tracts of land and many other things besides?'

"To this they replied that whatever people possess they have purchased at the cost of their strength, their soul, their freedom, their very life. But he insisted that he wanted to possess whatever seemed to him beautiful and desirable, and to keep all this as his very own without sharing it with others.

"For a long time they argued with him and then realized from his words that in his own eyes he appeared to be the first and only creature on God's earth, neither recognizing nor indeed being able to recognize any rights outside of himself. They shuddered when they saw how he was deliberately condemning himself to everlasting loneliness among men. He knew neither race, nor mother, no heroic deeds, and no peaceful occupation. He had neither herd nor home, nor mate, and he did not even feel the want thereof!"

In the distance, on the seashore, arose the merry ripple of a girl's laughter intermingled with the melting tenor of a gipsy song. The others regularly filled the rests in his rhythmical singing. The tender sheaves of melody rose and fell in the air, disappearing suddenly, as though someone had caught them in their flight and carried off this aerial booty to distant lands.

"When the elders saw that they could do nothing else with him, they deliberated again to determine the proper punishment. But this time their deliberation did not last so long, for that same wise elder who up to this time had said nothing about the penalty, now spoke up: 'Wait! The punishment already exists. And a most fearful punishment it is, the like of which has not been seen for many thousands of years. His punishment is within himself, inexorable and unescapable. Let him go free that he may live on — this is his punishment!'

"And thereupon a miracle took place. Out of a clear and cloudless sky there suddenly crashed a peal of thunder. The heavenly powers had confirmed the wise elder's judgment. The bystanders bowed their heads and each went to his home. But he, the eagle's son, whose name was henceforth Larra (which means abandoned, exiled), laughed loudly and boisterously at his judges and went forth a free man. — Lonely and free was he, just as his father had been. Yet his father was not a human being! And Larra began to live his wondrous life — free as an eagle. Often he appeared in the settlement of the race of giants, robbing them of their cattle and beautiful maidens; — whatever he desired for his pleasure was his pitiful victim. People shot their arrows at him, yet his body could not be pierced, for it was shielded against death by an invisible armor of retribution. He was quick, rapacious, strong and terrible. Rarely did anybody come face to face with him. He was seen for the most part from a distance. And whoever caught sight of him shot as many arrows as he possessed or was able to spare. And for many long years he roamed alone and companionless through the haunts of men.... Yet we mortals cannot endure unending joy; we cannot be happy in constant and unalloyed pleasure, for such pleasure loses all its value in the end, and then we begin to long for pain.... And so it once happened that he came close to the people, and when they were about to attack him he remained motionless, making no effort whatsoever to defend himself. Thereupon one of the people realized what he desired and he cried, 'Do not touch him! He wants to die!'

"And they all restrained themselves, for there was not one among them who wished to set him free from his evil lot of eternal life. They refrained from laying hands on him, but stood around and mocked him. Larra, however, trembled at their laughter and fumbled for something that was hidden in his bosom. Grasping it convulsively he rushed upon the men — with a stone in his uplifted hand. They avoided his attack but refused to strike back. Thereupon he fell upon the ground, weeping and weary, and they stood about gazing at his prostrate form. Seeing this he snatched a knife that had fallen upon the ground from one of the men during the struggle, and plunged it into his breast. But the knife snapped at the hilt as though it had struck against a stone; and once more he fell upon the earth, and in despair beat his head violently against it. The earth merely yielded, leaving a hollow where his head had struck against it.

" 'He cannot die!' joyfully cried those who had witnessed

all this. And they went away leaving him all alone. He lay upon his back and this is what he saw: High against the heavens like two black dots flew two mighty eagles. And he, a human being, lay there helpless upon the ground; and in his human eyes there was such deep longing, such endless, overwhelming sorrow that they could drown out the happiness of the entire race of mortals. And from that time on unto this very day he has been seeking for death — always alone, always in vain. And everywhere you can see him, seeking everywhere. . . . You saw him but a little while ago. . . . He is nothing but a shadow now, and a shadow he will remain forever. Now he understands neither the speech nor the actions of men. . . . He no longer knows what it is to live and the secret of death will forever remain locked against him. He merely wanders and seeks, seeks and wanders. His life is no life and the hope of death no longer smiles upon him, and no rest nor welcome can he find among men. Thus has God punished man's overweening pride!"

Old Isergil sighed and then became silent, while her head sank down on her breast.

I looked at her. Sleep was overpowering the old gipsy, and I pitied her. The latter part of her story had burst forth in loud, almost threatening tones, and yet her words rang with a timid and slavishly humble undertone.

A song arose in the darkness on the seashore. A most wonderful song it was! First an alto rang through the night, — a young girl's voice, singing the first measures of the melody. Then a second voice took up the same song from the very start while the first voice continued the melody, a few measures in advance of the second singer. Then a third, a fourth, and a fifth voice took up the same song, and each new voice began like the second, a few measures after the one previous to it, and continued the song through to the end. And suddenly a chorus of men's voices rang out, singing the self-same melody from the beginning, harmonizing and supporting the other singers, yet not in the least drowning out their voices. A fugue in the steppe! — Born among the common folk and sung by the common folk!

The melody was wonderful. Each female voice rang sweetly and distinctly out of the interweaving strands of music. It was as if many-colored rills were chasing and tumbling out of the air over a steep precipice and then swinging and melting together into a stream of exquisite melody. The voices rushed into this stream, submerging themselves within its depths and then with a ripple of laughter bubbling up on the surface again. One after another they tumbled pure and bright as crystal, and then rose once more into the heights. And the harmony, too, was wonderful. The male voices sang in a different and more simple rhythm, without any ornament or vibration, — somewhat heavy and melancholy, as though they were telling a tale of sorrow, — while the female voices, overtaking each other continually, seemed to be forevermore hastening to tell the same tale to their companions, — yet a tale that was no longer sorrowful but filled with the merry ringing of silvery fairy bells.

And this melody rose higher and higher until it overwhelmed the moaning of the sea.

ST. MARY'S COLLEGE OF MARYLAND
ST. MARY'S CITY, MARYLAND

47575